Paulie's Passover Predicament

For Caleb, of course! — J.S.

To all the fantastic children of this beautiful
world, because a child's smile is the most
precious thing we all have. — B.V.

© 2018 by Jane Sutton
Illustrations copyright © 2018 Lerner Publishing Group, Inc.

KAR-BEN PUBLISHING, INC.
A division of Lerner Publishing Group, Inc.
241 First Avenue North
Minneapolis, MN 55401 USA
1-800-4-KARBEN

Website address: www.karben.com

Main body text set in Cantoria MT Std Semibold 16/22.
Typeface provided by Monotype Typography.

Library of Congress Cataloging-in-Publication Data

The Cataloging-in-Publication Data for *Paulie's Passover Predicament*
is on file at the Library of Congress.
ISBN 978-1-5124-2096-8 (lib. bdg.)
ISBN 978-1-5124-2097-5 (pbk.)
ISBN 978-1-5124-9844-8 (EB pdf)

LC record available at https://lccn.loc.gov/2016059657

Manufactured in the United States of America
1-41265-23237-5/31/2017

Paulie's Passover Predicament

Jane Sutton   Illustrated by Barbara Vagnozzi

KAR-BEN
PUBLISHING

Paulie the moos-ician rushed through his morning practice in his basement studio. Usually he played longer, but today he had lots to do.

"Passover starts tonight!" he exclaimed. And Paulie wanted his Passover seder to be perfect!

Paulie went to the grocery store early. He couldn't wait to buy everything he needed for his perfect seder.

He had just put boxes of matzah into his shopping cart when he saw his friends Sally and Irving.

"Happy Passover, Paulie!" said Sally.

"See you tonight!" said Irving.

Paulie chose two candles for the table, and he filled his cart with *lots* of grape juice. After all, every guest would drink four glasses at the seder.

Once he got home, Paulie started cooking.

"Delicious!" he said, smacking his lips as he tasted each dish.

Paulie set the table for his friends.

He hummed happily as he placed
the matzah cover over the matzah.

"Perfect!" he thought.

When Paulie's friends arrived, he jumped up and down with excitement.

"Everything looks lovely, Paulie," said Irving.

"The food smells wonderful," added Horace.

"The candles are very 'you,' Paulie," said Evelyn.

"The matzah cover is quite unusual!" exclaimed Sally.

Then Paulie's friends all stared at the seder plate.

"I see you have an extremely large egg on your seder plate," said Moe.

"Yes," said Paulie, beaming. "An egg is a sign of new life. I used an ostrich egg to make sure everyone could see it."

"Why does the salt water look like pepper water?" asked Sally.

Paulie explained, "The salt water is like the tears of our ancestors when they were slaves in Egypt. But I added some pepper so my pepper wouldn't be jealous of the salt."

Paulie wasn't sure, but he thought he heard some giggles.

"Um . . . is that *charoset?*" asked Evelyn. "To remind us of the bricks and mortar our ancestors used to build the pyramids when they were slaves for Pharaoh?"

"Yes," said Paulie. "I made it with apples and yummy chopped pine cones."

"I think it is supposed to have apples and chopped walnuts," Evelyn said gently.

Irving asked, "Where's the parsley...
the Passover sign of spring?"

"Oh," said Paulie, "instead of parsley,
I used grass! Grass is my favorite green thing!"

Paulie wasn't sure, but he thought he heard
some chuckles.

"But Paulie," said Moe. "I don't see the *maror,* to remind us of the bitterness of slavery."

"It's right here!" Paulie said. "I remembered that maror is horseradish. So I carved a radish in the shape of a horse!"

"A horse-shaped radish instead of horseradish?!" Horace exclaimed with a guffaw.

"Paulie, dear," said Sally. "I don't see a lamb bone on the Seder plate. Remember? Our ancestors ate lamb on Passover."

"A lamb bone?" said Paulie. "I thought it was supposed to be lamb's wool!"

By now Paulie's friends were roaring with laughter.

Big tears formed in Paulie's big eyes.

"We're sorry, Paulie," said Moe, hugging his friend.

"Your seder plate *is* a little different," said Sally, "but each thing still reminds us of the meaning of Passover—in a Paulie way."

Paulie cheered up. He loved saying the blessings, asking The Four Questions, and telling the Passover story. He loved the tasty food. He loved dipping his hoof in grape juice as he and his friends recited The Ten Plagues.

Paulie asked Sally to hide the *afikomen*.

When it was time to look for the afikomen, Paulie really wanted to be the one to find it. That would make up for his seder plate mistakes! Now where could it be?

Under a table he found a missing hat.

Behind the couch he discovered
a long-lost stuffed animal.

But where was the afikomen?

He decided to look in the basement.
He searched under his drum set and in the
laundry basket.

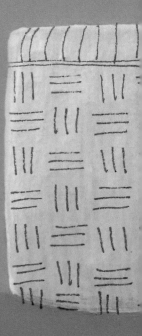

He looked in the dryer.
There it was!

Paulie clomped up the basement steps with the afikomen in his teeth. He pushed the door with his hoofs and antlers, but the door wouldn't open!

He bellowed for help, but his friends were having so much noisy fun searching for the afikomen that nobody heard him.

Paulie sank down on the steps. His first Passover seder was not perfect at all. He had used the wrong foods on the seder plate. And now he was stuck in the basement.

"What a predicament!" he thought.

Suddenly he had an idea.
He knelt down and carefully slid
the afikomen under the door.

A moment later, the basement door flew open, and Paulie burst out, free.

"Paulie! There you are!" all his friends exclaimed.

"You found the afikomen, Paulie!" said Horace. "You get a reward!"

"I don't need one," said Paulie. "My reward is being free, like our ancestors on Passover. And that's enough for me!"

Paulie, with his fine moos-ician's voice, led all his friends in singing the song *Dayeinu*:

"If God had only taken us out of Egypt, it would have been enough. Dayeinu."

"If God had only given us the Torah, it would have been enough. Dayeinu."

"And it's enough that we are all here together celebrating Passover in freedom—especially me!" said Paulie.

"*Dayeinu!*" said his friends.

About Passover

Passover is a spring holiday that celebrates the exodus of the Israelite slaves from Egypt. The holiday begins with a festive meal called a seder. Symbolic foods recall the bitterness of slavery, the haste in which the Jews left Egypt, and the joy of freedom. Children ask The Four Questions and look for the hidden piece of matzah—the *afikomen*—at the end of the meal.

Jane Sutton grew up in Roslyn, New York, where she began writing stories and poems at a young age. Jane is also a writing tutor and teaches a community education class for adults about how to write for kids. She, her husband, and her grown children live in the Boston area.

Barbara Vagnozzi loves illustrating for children, especially inventing funny animals. Her illustrations have appeared in children's books throughout the world. She enjoys giving workshops and presentations, where she can tell stories to little ones near her home in Bologna, Italy.